Dark Sunshine

mercuri serene

To anyone who cares to read this

Table of Contents

Part I:

the gloom sky

Black Curtains

I'm disappointed that I couldn't control

I wasn't strong enough to push open,

the black curtains in my mind

Letting my thoughts be seen by the audience

Cause now that the curtains are open and the lights
are shining

It's too late

The audience now gone

The black curtains start to slowly close and hiding
my thoughts again

I'm standing there wondering

Why can't I have theses curtains under control

Feels

I just want to close my eyes

Lie down in bed

With my dreams in head

Wanderin'

Hummin' my favorite sad melodies

Keeping myself from crying first thing in the
morning

Forgotten

Behind someone's else memories

When you remind every grain of detail is frightening

The feeling hits and crashes against my skull

Vision gets impaired

Now black out vision

Eye lashes brush the dark

Dreaming of the place of success

streSS

I just wanted to talk

I'm trying to be brave

I just wanted to be sure

But I'm scared

Scared, I'm never gonna have another chance

Crying, crying

Heart racing, tensing up

As my solar plexus churns

Now the time

To converse is here

Why

And I can't contemplate

What am I doing?

Why am I so attached

Oh, I am trying to train my mind

Biting my pencil, thinking

Wondering why and how

About everything now

The past, present, and future

Why am I doing this to myself

SAD art

Hates the world she lives in

Feels lost and torn

Trash by the sea

Unwanted, but before once used

***

As she sits in this room

With paper and pen

Doing what she knows how to

Staring out into blankness

About to risk her whole heart for her art

Her visionary mind, opened but lock closed for the
wrong reasons

Finding the key in other arts

Heavenly clouds, fluffy and engulfing

Going through the gates of imagine and finally land
on the paper

Idk

I don't know what to say

There are words in the space of my head

The reasons you are looking for

Words connect to sentences

They don't make sense

Emotionally manipulating

Life with parole

No control of the spinner of the game of my life

Terrified of the unknown

Follows the rules, takes these footsteps it whispers

I

Remind you of an unkept lawn

Not fitting into the perfect white fence

Not fitting into that house you built

Out of a sexual selfish society

My gender very much out of the two-party system

Attraction to these people, undeclared

But romanticize a certain type of romance
occasionally

While being chemically imbalanced emotionally and
mentally

Reminding you of those people's disdain

unwanted Flower

Looking around the beautiful translucent room

Filled with all types of energies and flowers

Seeing all these connections

Never going to be towards me

Nonetheless feeling pure beauty

But beastly unwanted by this society and my
attractions

So I ran to a marble bathroom

I stare into the mirror of dread

It's surrounded by many flowers

Some welting. Some lively

I examine the welting flowers

A lovely rose

Once as red with passion and romance

Now turns dark and hunch over

Without any of its standardized look, no one will
want the flower with no care

So it falls from its life line stem

Dying without the touch of love from anyone else

The deadly feeling of being unwanted rips apart the
pedals of self confidence

Exposed

A split of a second

The snap of my neck

Seen in a summer dress

The need to cover up

Drained in discomfort

In the middle of summer

Cold thoughts to cover up in heated weather

Hope

I want to feel the hurt nerves sting in my left arm

As I write with the right

Writing while sleep depressed from the anxious
monsters

I can finally feel something

All this numbness engulfing my control center

Can I now wring out tears

Or snap out of this hyper focus on figuring out the
monster's plans

Having now in their shackles

I can't even use the bathroom in my own home

Can't bear to look myself dead in the mirror

Wishing it was at least raining on the other side
of the reflexive glass

Its sound is sleepy but scary

Dark and gloomy like my mind

Time to burn some candles and wish and wish

Write and write and write

'Til feeling dangerously hopeful becomes reality

****

*Running round in my home with my favorite melodies
in the air and a poetry book in hand*

silent cry

This cloud won't pass through

It has been brewing for weeks on end

Now heavy and dark, over this hill

The cloud gently disappears away, before it could
rain

Before the rain could flood my mind

And leaks out my eyes

distorted dream

Uncomfortable silence is so overrated

I have to go back and go set change

As I walk away, I just want to scream

And go back to sleep

As I drift into an abyss

To this place that's a look like

The footsteps faintly echo behind me

I take to turn

Face to face with a muscled ghost

Then I become one with wind, as the ghost throw me
back

Scream, scared

As my mind go stale and static

Someone runs in, ready for battle

And that's when I knew

From peace to panic

Unfocused from sleep

My eyes still bugged

Trying to figure out the clues

Still confused

Socializing

Trying to catch a glance of happy

Blending in like the colors of a rainbow

Sick and still of emotions to even bother to try to
conversate again

Overreaction at fault

These people down here don't understand me

Will not see through me

Not worth the time for me to explain, clear the air

Or am I just afraid

Too dumb to bare

Too brainwashed to care

Life is far away from fair

Still in the dark down here

Earth smells

These screens illuminate the night

Still hope to escaping this place

Out of nowhere, somewhere

I have to catch the dream, but I'm stuck with this
cold glass of despair

Numb, now frozen in time

Sleepy but woke

Too desperate to feel

Love and care

Under the sea of trauma

Looking for someone to help me swim

But all there is are butterflies, the soft dragons
to carry me away

Finally saved

Breathe in and out they say

But not the flying creatures

But these people...

They don' t know that I'm suffering now more than
ever before

The indecisiveness and confusion

We want my ear now

A sharp knife through this conversation, tension is
thick

But maybe I'm just not into this

An alien stuck on this land

Sometimes there are guns pointed towards my way

This isn't a safe place

The game of tug of war in my brain will not end

These people here don't understand my pain

Enough of this game

But I can't lie and lay here in the cover of my
fortress

I want to fight to feel

Ever so lonely if I flight this brawl

I have to please the gunmen away most days and
nights

I don' t want to fly from the light of life

I had enough of this game

Hell in a classroom pt. 1

I feel the twitches, impulses

The dryness in my mouth

You might see panic in my eyes

I start to drift away

Back into my deep mind in a world I'm try so
desperately to escape

Just to hide from the monsters outside

I can't concentrate on words of the lesson

And before I know it, the bell rings

It's time to go into yet another ordinary
battlefield

Hell in a classroom pt. 2

In a group of four

With these boys that I don't know

Staring though my guard wall as it begins to thicken
with opacity

They proceeding to finish today's application

With no intent in wanting my involvement

The overwhelming panic streams through my body

△   The smell of science fire △

Mixed with the need to escape through the door

But frozen in place, so I use my phone

Forgetting I'm still in school

The phone magnetically attracts the teacher to sneak
up behind me

I hear a whisper of my name

I'm stuck between a truth and a lie

Should I trust this teacher, I have no valid reason
to lie

This causes my skin to itch and peel and it hurts
outside and inside

He walks away from the stale air of our
"conversation"

As I close my eyes, I am instantly drowning

Feeling my mentality spiral out of my grasp

Black streams carve into brown stone

With every tick of the analog clock, an ounce of
hope

Forgetting that I'm still in this hellhole

I'm going to be able to leave

The ring of release echoes through the classroom

Fight and flight

From this day, I had thought was this spark of
anxiety

Turned into an immense fire

That a splash of escapism wouldn' t fix this

Which burns a hole through strength to keep fighting
these day to day fights

Hell school

You cause me pain

My back hurts

My mind races

My eyes are tense

Those five minutes are precious

The thirty minutes even more

Trying to help me go through these gates of hell

While my mind tries to prepare for another battle

Ready to survive

In this cell I'm afraid to even drink water

My confidence extinguishing as the time goes by

Wrongly accused

Wanting a voice but can't behind these fiery bars

Controlling me

The devil's friends want me to stay

Guarding me to never to escape

I am the bonfire of a fire ring

It really sucks when you're happy

Walking into a building and become contained

Eyes stuck on me like a fly on honey

The sounds of footsteps crash around me

While my mind tries to prepare for another battle

Ready to survive

compliment

You can't even handle a compliment

He whispers from the back of my mind

His home, his cave

Dark and cozy I have to say

You do you feel so embarrassed and scared

Eyes in terror

He laughs a loud, echoes even louder

I try to not hide

They are lying

He smiles and mutters

You better hide that frown

My turn to return a halfhearted smile

Growing Pains

Too nostalgic

Make me want to cry

Back when I didn' t care about the others

Back when I didn' t live in the shadows

Cast by the demons

They were just bored and fascinated by this mind

My early experiences of life as their feast

Then they gain their fuel to then make this fire

Hearing the meetings of these demons

Wishing that the fire will clear so I can experience
the rest of my elements

Mother Nature

Every word I say falls out my mouth like acid rain

I don't mean any harm

The elements of my environment

The poison in my mind

People continue to pour ever so timely

They don't understand the way I work

They curse my name when it starts to rain

Rain Rain Rain

Ruining the land

I just couldn't hold the rain inside my brain

The clouds full then the thunder and lightning a
roar

Then again, I just can't control my rain

Raining Painfully

Creatures have this love hate relationship with rain

Whether it's a light shower or a windy downpour

They curse it in vain

Rain can either be downer or an upper

Same with pain

We have this love hate relationship with pain

We can't watch it from afar or endear close up

We can't swim or drown in it

Let it full our bodies with its cleansing, nurturing
properties

Both completely natural

Same with rain

So why not just embrace the pain it rains into your
life

Shouldn' t they both be just accepted as happiness
and sunshine

save

Wanted to be there so you don' t have to be so
scared

She has been dreading to feel those twelve words

Flow out of his mouth

Shower down on uncatered flower pots instilled in
her mind

Bloom with what will bring the world to its knees

To make her heart skip and jump a beat of life

The purest way he can save her

You Don't Know What It's Like

You don't know what it's like to pluck lashes out
of the lash line

Subconsciously rid the internal pain inside the
brain

The pain causes your eyes close and streams start to
crave your face

In the dark, in the walls of hell

The trauma and old memories flash in the back of the
eyes

You don't know what it's like

To be so dehydrated

From trying to find the water to flush it away

But in the light, the halls of heaven

New beginnings, new sense of identity

Replenished with the water

To finally rid the annoyance and struggle of this
mental pain

You don' t know what it's like

~~To bear the strength to try to change a way of
thinking to live a happier life~~

An Open Case

Still on the chase to find this criminal

Suspected on taking my mind

Lose sleep for the thought of it

Controlling my headspace to shut down and weep

Just want this case to be closed

Brain Surgery

I wish I can cut up my brain

Rearrange and examine

Curiosity always in the air

Feed these unwanted, damage pieces to the wolves

They hold the memories that sadden me

The inner vines, comforting my mind

But every so softly trying to use it

Slightly having a grip and squeezing me

Travels down from my brain to my throat to my toes

Wrap around as if it's cold

Every so swiftly

Until my mind now can't fight or flight

Now engulfed in a plan to get out of this hold

The leaves brush my mind to be silent, still stuck
head to toes

The vines tighten their grip, electric anxiety air
still in my lungs

Struggling to breathe out, panic pools up my eyes

up all night

Waking up into a room of light

Your eyes will want to hide as they will burn and
hurt

Close them to block the strain weather

As promises and thoughts try to peek inside

Annoyed in how they make you feel

Rubbing your eyes as if this will make them feel
better

But the ache is still there, this brightness is
condescending

You will gladly take darkness

The rain and unsureness

Wanting to stay in the dark drowning cloud

Rest and recover from lasts nights weather

shamefully hot

She sits in dirty sun

Skin feels of dry leather

Insecurity travels though this roasting air

Through her ear and into her mind

It's not her fault

Nobody sharing their cool shade

No person there to help

It's not her fault

These people want to punish her, make her feel lost

As it is now dusk

The sun has its eye half open

Those people are gone from sight

As she escapes, looking straight into the different colors,

she drifts to another conscious

Feeling those same people crawl and scrap their way into her dreams

It's dark and lonely in here

Tossing and turning her angry and frustration

Breathing and fighting in the world of lone consciousness

Hoping these people stop their invasion

Magicland

Over the rainbow she goes to a land of purity and
clarity

Where one can be free and far from any fears

Build bonds and bridges with people that she can
hide from

Where she can cry with and feel their support

These bonds and bridges can never be broken

That is what she and the rest thought...

Until one day, a lovely dark blue cloud, with a hint
of violet sparkle

That had covered the land with its unique shape

As the rest of the people fairly disappear

She stayed in place

There she watches this cloudy creature rise over the
rainbow

Both frozen in warm weather

She watched the mystical yet delightful creature
float slowly to her

Shrinking in size as it moved

The eye of this cloud creature stare into her eyes

Both pair full of melancholy

The cloud thunders in agony

Which in turn, startles the girl into questioning

How can these people just run and hide, watch from
inside

Now the cloud form droplets in distress

Poisoned of sadness

They fall down more and more on the ground

Puddles turn into rivers that crave the land

The girl becomes soaked and stain

Empathy rivers down the hills of her face

too MUCH

I can't think straight

Your questions and ideas are like clouds in the sky

Light at sight but heavy with the intent of getting
a solution

You cloud my mind and they damage it

What am I trying to do is my only question

As if I'm drowning, inhaling water

I can't think straight, I'm getting painfully full

Your suggestions are like an anchor hooked to my
feet now

Struggling to escape the indecisiveness

I can be tired, quite frankly I am

The struggling shoes I wear in this deep blue place

Letting the water become one with my body again

I just can't run away and try to seek a place to
hide

In a globe, stuck to sticking to camouflage

Trying to find an escape, being a bit unhealthy

Physically and mentally connected as one

Disappointing my body

Breaking me soulfully

Bleeding out for empathy and help

Screaming for the answers for all this rotten
rubberish to go away

Whilst trying to run away under the silvery sky

Letting the rain comfort and cover me

The water in my body is magnetic

Being pulled by the clusters of ice water in the sky

Trying to have the mental peace whilst now I am
cuddling the clouds

Tornado

Its hit him like a tornado

The words swirls and spin

Around his mind

The sirens, going off

Panic rises to the clouds

He needs to find shelter

In the middle of this windy storm,

it's nearly impossible to survive

Yelling out to these words to let go of him

To unravel their spinning effect on him

Escape

Looking to order some ice skates

Get far away from this place

To a frozen lake

Just imagine

Trying to keep balance upon arrival

Stopping to look underneath at the frozen wonderland

Its ever so frigid in frozen air

Warming, lively marine and greenscape underneath

Between marine and me

Polar opposites, but identical needs

Alike, wondering and worrying about having the
outside intruding in

Wanting to be sane and safe

The sounds of skates scrapping

The flutter of the many fish

The vibrations flow up and through my feet

Both the same, surviving

Opposites

Warm but chill in temperature

One with libs and ones with fins

I'm just wanting to escape

The smell of salt ice and chilled air

Under ice, they are just wandering

Scared

Scared to share

Why am I here at this hearty morning meal

Lovely scenery

Lively people

Yet too timid to talk

He whispers to me to be quiet

Honey and syrup keep my lips as one

My tongue struggle to move

The words of giving up echo through my head

The volume deafening

People can see my eyes squinting

Then the man in my head again

Softly spoken this time

Wanting plentiful food

Packing my plate

He is in control now

He knows I lack appetite

As the uneasiness of this event fuels off my
insides,

people around pleased with normalcy

While depersonalization orbits me,

the man shouts in my head that he's trying to help
me

I feel my control soak away like butter on warm
toast

Walls

I feel the walls form

As I stare out into space

But the planets and galaxies don' t appear

Those walls try to block thoughts out

With every crash and wave of salty waters

Produced by my mind

As the water overfills

Throat closing soon, a panic sign states on one of
the walls

These walls form with every gain gallon of sad
frustration

Feelings start to brew a black hurricane

Then these walls start to weaken with every rumble
and movement...

waking up

Waking up with the usual cup of headache and sore
eyes

Lying back down in my duvet,

that's soaked from the tears the night before

The sun filled bedroom rays through the bad mood of
last moon

The steam of my cup blocking the glass windows,

for my tired visionary organs

Needing them to help distract me from the panic of
today's general society

Alone in the Forest

Floating on the smell of loneliness

A bit of evergreen mixed in there as well

And the sound of my breathing

The crunch of dead leaves as I walk

Uncertainty fills my brain

As my body feels the chilled earthy air

And then tenses inside my body,

pleading for a way to leave

The shadows

The shadows of the past block their minds,

blocking their vision and perception of time

They beg to have light to see

To fight the shadows of the painful past

Then just when they were on the verge of giving up,
lights appear

The lights

They begin to see feel future

They start to feel present of hope crawl into their
minds

The blinding lights start pushing back the terrible
sinful shadows

Present of hope begun to feel new

Beginning as the shadows disappear, they can see and
think clear for themselves

Without the shadows guileful tactics

They can survive and grow from the lights of future

talking to the moon

Sitting on a wooden bench

Spiked wood

As the moonlight casts

The spotlight is on

It's time to speak

But scared the words aren't going to glow;

though the sleeping souls

Alone outside at night

This is a sign from the night child

To thrive in the dark perhaps

Remember this scenery will change, everything will
continue to evolve

Either have disappearing optimism or some sort of
mortal peace

As the moonlight flickers as it senses the change in
solitude

The moons glow enchants my soul

Across its belly in the sky spells

It's your time to speak now

Part II:

the moon is revolving
and revealing

Unwired but Wired

Reality from the usual

Lost in the unusual

Sold lies and paradise

Gain fear and want to hide

Baited and played by the simulation of one's mind

Many minds controlling, many minds controlled

Because there's levels in knowledge

Experiences and characteristics

Making everyone unwired

Because we are all the same,

in need to live and survive

Sadly, the pressure and unawareness are wired into
some minds

Causing hatred to the ones who don't follow,

nor copy and paste

If not harmed or trapped then they won't nudge

It's up to you to fix the wires

Life is divergent for everyone

It's up to you if you want to be falsely wired

Cut them away with your installed information

Brainwashed

Their heads are above the troubled water

Seeing their way to the beach of desire

It seems everyone around aren' t drowning and start
swim with no problem

Yet after arrival

No one talks about the survival

I yet to know why

I'm still struck in water

My eyes above, clear vision of this beach

But my airways fill with these problems

You may ask how I know about the people who survived

Because no one talks about the troubles

They stand on the shore glorifying their struggles

Now there are people still in the whirly waters,
with their foot stuck in the mud underneath

Eyes just above, mouth closed with sunken breath

Slowly we start to embrace the struggle with no need
to wobble

As the waves push the pain away

Then suddenly the water is wrinkle free

The mud snatches me and some others

Mouth opened, hit with a clear vision to an
underwater world

No need of struggles

On the back of a string ray shows on that beach of
the survived

Their heads fill with water and leaks from their
eyes

They start to follow, wobble and fall in line

Stop hiding

Stop trying to hide your honesty with apologies

And stop trying to brain wash me

Stop with the childish lies and shallow greetings

Stop hiding from me

Start with a warm truth

Cause that' s what I' ve been giving you all

To the Frenchman

I lying on my side in my bed

When I hear a sound

It wakes me from my sleep

It's him on my mind

Instantly, my body fills with shame and regret

To reminiscing to when my heart flipped and my
insides flutter

When I saw your name across my screen

Amazed by how you'd remembered everything I said

Never bothered by the awkwardness of my conversation
starters

Our small talks helped me through the social dread
of a school day

Still stuck wishing on the moon

Just to have to experience your ghostly leave

Now stuck in the bittersweet honey of needing to
lose you

From a love that I thought I desire

To a love that I need

Turning my imperative ghost into my valuable mortal
blessing

10ve <3

What is it?

Why is it so important to the people's minds

Addictive, fluid, and comforting even in the coldest
of winters

Yet complex, confusing and broken

The many forms and ways to express it

Each person in their unique way

Yet it's all so foreign to me

So, why does it have such control over us?

What makes it a priority to living energies?

Because of the naturalness of energy attraction

Or the fear of love's contraries

But I completely understand why people want this
love life

But first I have to realize why it isn't present in
my life

Because love itself is lively

It can strengthen your magnetism of romantic energy
or drown your vitality

That's what makes love so desirable and potent

But then again, it's all divergent to me

you NEVER had ONE?

You all have something I don't have

It's quite embarrassing to say aloud

Brings bags filled with insecurities to my door

And waves of loneliness at times

Stay up to the late of night as the waves crash
against my eyes

Thinking why you all were surprised by my answer

"...no..."

Her Spring Dream

The calmness of her voice

Sweet rain hits the ceiling

The smell of rain rinsed honeysuckles

A rinsed spring morning

Her voice melts her brain

But can awaken a savory thought

Honey dipped eyes capture her

She had the woman in her world

Her escape to the spring dream

Birds speak to the flowers and trees

They blossom ready for the sun and its warmness

And the kindness of creatures

A spring break from her war in the red gates of
darkness

Fight and flight

As they lie down on the sun kissed ground

She's done with fighting

The other girl grabs a bucket of berries

Picks a garish of flowers to decorate

"Fuel your brain," she stares

A spell put on the berries only she knows

Wanting the woman to stay close

To never to go back to war

Feeling her courtesy to protect her

Because that's what she's done for her

Now with that in mind,

the woman is trapped in her world

Tenderness

Light the fire inside

One or two bodies lie beside

Let one's emotions boil and steam

Lovely and cozy underneath

The whispers of subconsciousness

The steam of the boil finally rises and escapes

Out the minds through the air ever so suavely

The space around is silenced and soundproof

They feel nothing else matters, the world disappears

In this moment, the fire dies down

Sounds and worries of the world start to roar

They feel a sense of return to earth

with a pinch of old reality

To the return to societal war

Too tender for the outside world

PRESsUred in a Box

In this world of mine

Everybody has these labels to put on these boxes

Society's job

The pressure to stay and get in line, follow the
leader and get a pay out

The lack of fearlessness to change without hate and
violence

But in this world of mine

Filled with toxins and old times

Historic ties to our bloodlines

Many cultures and theories

So much societal gatekeeping

Having set regulations on organizing these boxes

But in this world I live in

Competition and comparison are just two of the many
unwritten pressures

Brave

Scared and scarred

As they sit in the open room

No roof, no doors, no windows

Nothing but rain shower

Then rumble and roar of the rain drops in the
ancient tile

So lively and loud

"Live life," he says

Looking into the eyes of sunshine

He and they stay

Soaked and sadden all of a sudden

"We have to obey," he whispers behind their ear

As his arms stretches around their body, with a
scent of hesitation

Comfort and freedom spread through both bodies

Then the puddled leaves on the ground

Around them capture tears for the rainbow above

As rain shower stopped

His arms snap back to his sides

The sound of secret fills their ears, the thought of
hiding very vigilant

As the forest trees strolls through, with confusion
and surprise in his eye

Now they know why he said we have to obey

"Brave" in confusion

I am listening to your voice

In a puddle of blankets and lush

Drowning in questions

I've been trying to swim to the top

Paddling the questions away

Swimming towards avoidance

Then to the sounds of the words

Come here

Your eyes pulling me in closer

Then in a blink

Desperation, admiration

Turns the struggling water to black ink

Ignorance to those feelings

But stained with the confusion

some boys don' t like me

Spending all my time

Finding and figuring out

Lost in my world of desires

Trying to fill the void of all of you

You all have hurt and damaged my way of thinking

Heightened anxiety fills my brain

Making me dizzy and distance

You all have some potion to fix me

Filled with cluelessness and apologies

mixed with unawareness of your damage

Parched from the unsure dislike you all have

I take a gulp of your potion and let it force the
pain to amplify

As its bothersome to bare inside, invisible tears
fill my eyes

Hypocrite

I have problems

I remind you of a certain man you used to love

He used to tell me we'd crash heads

The validity aged nicely

So go ahead and scream and whine

I don't have time to explain myself

To be told when to used my words

I admitted that I was wrong

But I have some news to pass on

You have problems, just as wrong

Headlined in bold print

You and him have some similarities

But he escapes his problems in the bottom of a
bottle

A down grade in personnel

A change in personality

Problems and actions affect the people he honors

Killing the relationships that were made of iron

Setting fire on these bridges

The flow of how they worked is now broken

I pushed the injuries away to fix it

Making my injuries worse trying to fix his

Call Me by My Name

Uncomfort mixed with a bit of distrust

Manipulation of wanting to be in control

Have no accountability for your actions

You repeatedly stroll in and out my heart,

my chest left open, bruised and sore

As the clock ticks away, we are short of time

To be pretending to care

Why bother

Trying to clear your submind

I'm stuck in a gated room of the both of you

Creating a tug of war

Needing to be liberated

Or is this all out of your confused mind

Clueless of what is going on in your life

Paranoia and revenge have leaked into your drink

Traveling through the blood that we both share

Uncomfort mixed with a lack of intellect

The things said through the cans of beer

Drugged induced or apathetic brain

Reminding you of someone you don't like

There only so much to do though a phone

The words you said to me scream back at me

in my awake and dormant mind for time to time

When something reminds me of you

I call out your name

Sick from the Toxins

My vibrations are at an all-time low today

As my annoyance and frustration to not be able to
express and compromise

That this isn't just your world

This home is just yours

And all the whimsical fountain water droughts out

Like my patience and there's no way to distract
myself from this torture

As my emotions build and block any good energy from
reaching me

That hinder me from overcoming this sea of sickness

Causing this sickness, this dizziness, ever so
drained of energy

So I close my eyes hoping help will be near

My eyes, my eyes, my eyes

My head, my head, my head

Both feel impaired

Feeling like I just been in a 12-round boxing fight

And then thrown through a brick wall

With every word you say

With every thud of every song, you blast aloud

Feels like a slap to the face

At this point

I just need you to know that things are going change

I need to drown in the sadness and sorrow, in the
state of giving up

To cleanse and rebirth into a new state of energy

You will be hard to forget

Not easy to forgive

But at the point, I'm done with the trespassing of
my boundaries

Degrading my existence

At this point, anger churns in my stomach

Turning into painful confusion

Causing me to lament my decision to end this taxing
relation

And to begin my cycle of solitude from you

Father Figures 1.0

This needs to change

Needing my answers

It's getting abhorrent

Why do I feel so empty

Yet so fulfilled with a life without you

The deadly liquid can' t live without you

Wishing you close your mouth and listen

Or that mindset of careless and bitterness of your
past before me

Now I'm left with the thought of you emptying your
life of me

Father Figures 2.0

Stepping on the glass of us

He has shatters what we built

Every day is sickly normal

For him

Yet annoyingly ordinary frustrating for me

Putting the needs of a damaged creature

Before your own

Sitting here anxiety torn

This creature doesn't have a care in the world

Fueling the creature what it wants

Making things worse

Losing your worth

Putting him on a throne where he doesn't belong

While it screams from the outside and the inside

Shatters the home with its strident voice

Sitting here as annoyance permeates the air

As he spits fake wisdom at others alike him

Under the LOUD music

In the chatter

Surrounded in a cloud of lovely smoke and beautiful
bottled liquor

In the chatter

I hear from up the hall

You scream what my mother so desperately screamed to
you the night before

In the chatter

I learn that you listen efficiently

I know because I hear from the tone of your voice

As the night goes on

That chatter dies and slows down was the drinks pour
over your speech

Another conversation ignites

But inside the cold car

To and from

Her natural frustration, her subconscious shouts out

Her body shows her

That your collateral chatter and choices

Your comfortability in drowning yourself and us in
booze

Is abusing

My final thoughts at the end of the night ride,

underheard by the snores of you and the sounds of
the bag of food you wanted

I whisper, "I know, I understand, I feel the same
way"

As the morning sun shine into my soul and wakes me

I sigh in empathic frustration

She needs to set her intentions in stone and stop
hurting herself emotionally

Listen to your heart and body

As manipulation cycles back

Again, she's trapped inside your world

Sorry

I don' t feel sorry for you

Or him

As I stave and dehydrate for respect

It angers me when I hear everyone loosing up and
laughing,

while my brain is in a tangled mess

While you constantly get abused emotionally

While I need to untangle the yarn and make something
with *this*

I'm in and out of conscience

I start to faint into guiltiness for giving up on
you

The more I observe this situation

The more I learn

The more I understand

I do feel sorry for you

As you are in and out of a freezing pit of self-
awareness and self-action

I'm hoping one day you just really listen to
yourself

your KING

It's disgusting the way you talk about her

Graphic and sexist

Downright degrading

Why do you want her next to you

Why don't you get the message she's trying to send
you

There's a child here

And there's a child in you

Growing disrespectful and demanding

Toxic masculinity made from childhood issues

But that shouldn't be an excuse

That in this house, in front and behind people

there's your unspoken sober rule, but spoken in
slurred speech

To submit to silence and service, to tolerate your toxicity

tired *eyeroll*

I'm sick of your comments

Sly and slimy

Slip and slide on this bench

Underneath the gray storm

The trees starting to look like their roots

The wind from your outbursts and your coldness to
emotion

Picking the life off these trees for boredom

Now the wind has them in its mitts

Twirl and whirl

Destroying our home

Trying to protect what's left of my peace and love
for this place

Toxic energy combines with mine

Needing to be detached

With the bench I'm sitting on is still intact

After the thinking battle in my mind,

unharmed and protected from my energy

My vision of gray hopelessness,

altering this reality with bright golden days,

when Ice cream in the little hand of me in May

Kissed by the sun and warmed with old yet young
memories

This distortion gets wiped away

The bench now debris

Rain drenched earth

With the leaves of your comments

Stuck to the ground of tonight and tomorrows

after my job interview

How are we so far apart but live so close

So close in the house of a worker's education

Seeing you all walk pass my motionless body

You all stroll down different paths that I never
knew existed

We're all growing into our society

How are we so far apart but live so close

As I'm struck watching and wishing we were closer

Experience together

This separation makes my desire to leave stronger

As I wake up during the cusp summer days

Lonesome peeps and creeps in my mental from time to
time

I start to admire at the sky at dusk

I start to connect the nighty stars

And found the outline of *you*

Wondering are you too in in the same space in
emotionally

But obviously there's a variation of being alone in
on a new stage of life

What are you doing to distract?

Drinking into unawareness and escapism

Smoking, inhaling false relaxion

Exhaling negative energy

Or are you even bothorod

No prudent to the situation

To our situation

Patience

So close to the light

Eyes closed

Warm fingertips and palms full of the energy of
abundance

The mini barks of a black dog and the birds sing me
awake

The room filled with solar energy

But with the sound of ignorance and image of a toxic
being
Switching to the dark ache and madness

The yelling and ordering for a damaged fool

A glance of my current emotions

A feel of the energy of my living space

There isn't enough light to get this energy to go
away

But I'll be patience

Capitol of Texas

I saw you and you saw me

Your eyes scared me to look away

But during that three second interaction,

I remembered all the convos we had

The many satirize jokes

But after those three seconds pass

You are gone

Gone to your way of purpose

With the person that glued your presence to me

This fRiEnD I had

You ran up to me with secrets

Wanting my ear to listen

It does what it is ask of out of love

Then you run away

Leaving me in dust

Left coughing and choking

I wanted to give advice

I'll just stay quiet

no judgement

You say that I'm that friend

That friend you can be yourself around

Lightning struck down on an acorn

Electricity written over my face

Never would have thought this would happen in clear
sky weather

These two words came to mind

No judgement

Sparks back that memory and that melody

I came to realize

Chill calm comfortable

You all think I am just that

But even with all those positive adjectives

In the back of my mind, a gentle poke of a finger,

I hear a whisper, *"no they' re lying"*

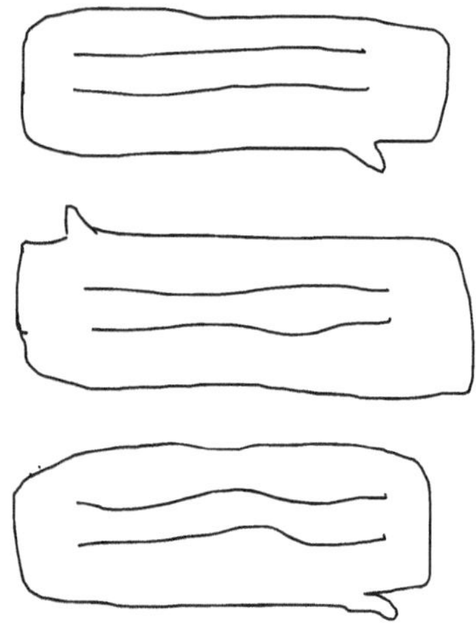

an END of our group calls

The randomness of laughs and loudness

Everyone's world colliding

So far away but ever so close

Yet so bored of all the roaring

Energy is being misplaced

Their people start to come back home

Roality soaks in

And those people are who they want to see

Then there's me

With the starvation for their normalcy

As noises of conversation mistakes start to run wild

Needing to be distracted yet again

as the noises of my household ascends in volume

Us after Highschool

Will we stay close

Everyday talk, randomness and

Different schools, different ways

Separation smelling quite stale

The scent of alone lingers still

Doubt, the drought of confident

The cracked floor of anxiety screams why

Bright blue to linty gray

Stare at the sky, trying to block my eyes

Black fills the outside

Losing where we were

Saturated of sorrow and sadness

I begin to drown in this water

As wide panic shoots through my body

✳   SURPRISE   ✳

A door slams right in my face reads,

THEY DONT NEED YOU

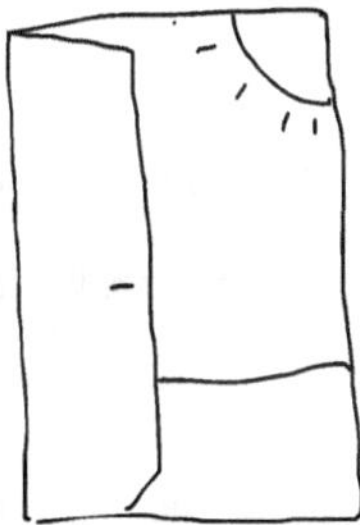

jealousy?

When you sit across the classroom

You hear me get something I don't get often

In return you beg for them to compliment you instead

From then and to now I realized

Your insecurity masked by the friendship I thought
we had

This isn't the first time your insecurity has
unmasked itself

It being trapped is causing you frustration

Masked insecurity causes jealousy for what you wish

You aren't the only person in the world to have this
problem

Certainly, not the last

With my intuition getting better over aged time

Our friendship ending was always inevitable

My higher power had been helping me see who you are

Because underneath all your perfect sweet image you
draw to these people

You are a broken hypocrite and a copy of a copy

OK BYE

You aren't afraid anymore

You left me torn

You are teaching me to live without you

The truth left a burn

I know you felt it

But it will heal eventually

Competition isn't friendship

I lack the energy to defend myself

You were intimidated

You hate that I knew your truth

You choose to competemand won by cheating

But I know I won honestly

***

With the universe's helping hands

A relieve of the rusty chains wrapped around my head

Now I'm finally done and complete

Without the demand of your toxic need of attention

Without the invisible cycle of owning you back

Especially my friendship

There are cycles in life

And this will come back to you

As my truth condensates from the fake water you pour

Your reality will hide behind the clouds

And the last words you said to me the title of this
poem

Roses

With a rose in hand

Drawn in the sand of the beach

Promises will never separate

There with the friends trying to train me

To adapt their perfect normalcy

*We are all nice and have no judgement, don' t you
see*

We never disagree on any pebbles at the sea

But in reality, they are reflecting their fears on
me,

trying to blend in, scared to voice their opinions

I scream out at the ocean

Throw the fish back into the ocean and let the
scorpion crawl in the sand

Staring at the lone moon in ocean mirror

With the strong waves of numbness

Crushing the burden to be the lifeguard of you all

I have to guard myself in the only way I know how

All the darkness of mental illness and untimely
sleep of my eyes

The decaying of age of the shore stones shows

Taking them in hand to be examined

Tossing them back into the ocean, I slowly walk
back to the shrub where I got the rose

With moisture of sea water left on the skin of my
hand

I splash on the second rose

As an apology for snatching its partner in nature,

Which kept them less alone, knowing how that felt
before

Watching the waterdrops rest on the petals

Wondering why I feel uneasy peace at the beach

Part III: the sun rise

The falling leaf

Every last vein

Shrinking day by day

The sweet summer sun diluted by the cool breeze of
autumn

Makes the leaf change its style and hue

As the leaf hangs on to its mother

The wind of routine growth softly guides the leaf

To land wherever it lands

Letting whatever weather pour on it

Being one with familiar ground

Let t in g G O

Breathing in blue and breathing out grey

The cool relaxation begins to stay

As the warm cerulean water washes away this rotting
unwanted substance,

that can bring a being to a forever sleep

The greyness of the sky through my eyes brought
sadness and frustration,

To exhale out the unnecessary need to pay attention
to my irrelevant deeds

Awake

It's still dark after waking up

With the shadows of needy people

The nastiness of people in society,

the friends that I thought were different

Old shadows in my mind

New shadows around my environment

A need to escape becomes stronger

The gate of solitary starts to budge open

Wanting to push down and away

The toxic feeling as it intensifies

In the back of my mind, the desire to stay in place

With only light in this room reads a sign of change

As my second mind immerse in peace

A new level of mind and matter

Forces the gates to open to acceptance

And the force of my beginning

Don't believe them

As a reminder to myself

I learned that people's perception of you isn't
always accurate

Because when I listened to all those perceptions of
me

I tried to live up to them

Believed them

So, I look at the myself in the mirror and see who I
am

I feel who I am

We all have our own brain and can define ourselves

People who wear these perceptions are the same
people who follow

Which is understandable

It's a natural thing organisms on this earth do

When in doubt, look about what's revolving around us

But back to my beliefs on people being labeled and
wired

This can hinder a person into not living for
themself

Trying to live up and believe these perceptions

Left to need unhealthy validations

Rescued

Stuck in the mud

Quicksand

The more I move, things stay the same

Until after a long sleep

A rope wraps around my hand

The sound of man-made wings travels through my brain

I grab hold of the rope

Moving out of the misery of constant struggle

Scared to look down at the destruction of the world
I was in

The futuristic breeze of this air will be snapshot
in modern memory

Hope pt. 2

Writing to these melodies

Feeling dangerously hopeful

Fresh morning leaves fall around

As the chilled wind blows my insecurities away as I
stroll through the wind,

I start to hear and see the autumn forest

Crisp with bright colors

The warm sun is the medicine needed

As I had awakened to read this thriller book to set
the scene

Disconnect to connect

There I stay still in place

As I close my eyes to enter a higher self

"I am who I want to be" , I say to the cotton
clouds

As I visualize my goals and desires

My nightmares start to become daydreams

Solitude

Sitting in this theatre

Enjoying the stars of rare company

In the space of realizing a disconnection in
constellations

Intuition whispers to me to keep guard of the black
holes in my physical environment

Emotions orbit around my mind

My energy slowly connecting with the universe

When the movie is over

The moisture of the late summer night air

Grips and sticks to me, trying to keep me in the
moment

But I start to evolve as my elements realign

I look up at the clear sky, through the window of my
outer space

And then look down at the nightly creatures as they
crawl over the human made ground

I hear distant chatter and normalcy of friends

As I close my physical eyes

Blocking my present vision

Inside my mind there's a message

It's time to leave them behind

my inner s p a c e

Here in the frigid cold ice land

Uncomfortable hat radiates off of me being lost and
alone

Transported

Here in the dry sandy desert

Cooked alive in an oven

Left scared and pressured

To another extreme to another

Both never admired

Deserted and nervous

Never content

Having the time to think

Making the most out of this time to breathe

Without the busy streets and responsibility to
connect and communicate

Transported to another extreme place

With

my inner space

Feeling vintage but young

Old soul, young heart

Young eyes surrounded by no sleep and many of mind
games

Soulfully feeling like I lived decades earlier

Everyone around me knows so much but so little

So little on why to live

So much on how to live

Feeling like I'm dying from young age

Filled with so much regret and nerves of desperation

Yet again, feeling old but young

Vintage soul, teenage heart

I anticipate the flutters of the butterflies carry
me to first love

As the butterflies decorate my hair

As I float to my soul's friend to have an old
romance

As I sit here with the stars of the night in
moonlight

Thinking to myself...

The elements we are all made of

Constantly needing to be balance

Because death is old destination

And life is young journey

Hygge

Looking at the moon

Feeling the power, it gives off

Close my eyes to see my dreams

Wild Heart crop top

Feeling ever so confidence on top of the high
vibrations

Letting the music move through my body

In a color I hate and love, red & pink

As I stare in the mirror of hell and beauty

Just like my body

My skin suede as the letters on the shirt I have on

The feeling between high and low is dazed

As I take the shirt off at night

Exposed, as if left in the wild dark,

loving the memory made from something I hate

Hygge pt. 2

As I stand in the rain, the leaves of brown, orange
and yellow fall around me

As the outside screens black and white

As I walk through a beaded curtain of cool water and
dying leaves

I spot a cluster of pink cone flowers

As I close my eyes, the image feeling instant energy
of comfort

Thankful

I will like to forgive everyone for hurting me

Some friends and some family

As the sand is marked by the hurtful words and
distressing memories of yesterdays

Wash away by the waves of tomorrows

Leaving me a clean surface to restart

I will forgive myself

For all the past bad habits

As I drown into oiled water, to be rescued on shore

As the moon rain cleans my skin and soul

I will like to thank everyone for healing me under
this full harvest moon

Because without the hurt, you wouldn't learn to heal

Reminders

I am enough

I am worthy of respect

I am worthy of love

I am a work of art

I am a creative soul

I inspire others

I am beautiful inside and out

I radiate positive energy inside and out

I am strong mentally and physically

I am better than my past

I forgive myself

My feelings are valid

I deserve the best

I can achieve my goals

I am successful in everything I do